Calculated
In
Color

A Dakota Maddison
Tattoo Shop Mystery
Book 2

This is a work of fiction. Names, characters, places, and incidents either are the product of the author's imagination or are used fictitiously. Any resemblance to actual persons, living or dead, events, or locales is entirely coincidental.

Copyright @ 2023 by Trish Arrowsmith

All rights reserved. No part of this book may be reproduced or used in any manner without written permission of the copyright owner except for the use of quotations in a book review. For more information, address: trisharrowsmithauthor@gmail.com

First paperback edition February 2025

Book cover design by Nirkri@fiverr

Dakota Maddison logo by @sirbro_ink.az

ISBN 978-1-961676-01-5 (paperback)
ISBN 978-1-961676-00-8 (ebook)

www.trisharrowsmithauthor.com

For all those following Dakota, Declan, and Diesel.

Thank you!

Chapter 1

I stayed up way too late enjoying the barbecue and bonfire with my friends. I hadn't seen any of them, except Falcon, since the week of my grand opening. This coming weekend is the fourth of July and I invited everyone to come celebrate the holiday with me. Last time they were all here, I focused all my attention on the shop's opening going smoothly and I was the prime suspect in a murder, so I used a lot of energy trying to clear my name. I'm looking forward to finally being able to spend quality time with them over the next few days.

I tried to take the entire week off, but I have one tattoo appointment scheduled for later this afternoon that the client and I scheduled months ago. Because the shop has been closed for the last two days, I'm going in early to give myself plenty of time to give it a thorough cleaning. Every time I close for more than a day, I find it necessary to scour every surface, the doorknobs, chairs, floor, and counters, to ensure the sanitary conditions. I put my windows down to enjoy the breeze on my drive over. The sun already sat high and the air hung thick with early summer humidity. After four months, it still brought me great joy driving over and seeing my shop, knowing how much effort I put into it. All traces of the spray paint someone used to brand me a murderer, just a few months ago, were gone and from the outside, it looked professional and welcoming. I sighed looking at the camera mounted above the door. It was one piece of the city I hoped to leave behind when I moved to such a small town. Due to the circumstances when I first arrived, I put it up for safety, but it felt out of place now.

    I dropped my keys and bag on the counter and started toward the back of the shop to turn the lights on. Despite being late morning, the shop remained dark without help from artificial lights. My foot connected with something on the floor, sending it rolling away. I stopped and looked down, needing a moment for my eyes to fully adjust. There were bottles of ink scattered across the floor, the organizer that I had previously fastened to the wall, now lay in pieces; shards of the thick plastic were flung in all directions.

"What the..." I stepped over a few bottles, still wanting the light so I could see what happened. Right before walking into the back room, I froze. A body lay motionless in the doorway, their head pointing toward me. "Not again." I pulled my phone from my pocket and turned on the flashlight. The light gleamed off a large knife protruding from the victim's back and a puddle of what appeared to be blue and purple ink and blood mixed in a nauseating form reminiscent of a painter's pallet on the floor.

So much for enjoying the festivities and quality time with my friends.

The fourth of July is my favorite holiday and I wanted to celebrate it with my favorite people. The excitement of them accepting my invitation had me so caught up, I forgot it was the busiest weekend of the year. The hotel and all the cabins on the lake booked out months in advance. Unwilling to give in so easily, I borrowed cots and air mattresses from everyone I could and my house became a makeshift motel with barely enough room to move around without bumping in to someone or stepping on them if they were sleeping. I enjoyed catching up with all of them last night, but since everyone was at my house, I felt bad about leaving them on their own so I could sneak off to go to sleep. Owning my own business, it wasn't often that I didn't get enough sleep, I worked on my own schedule, but I also got up early most mornings to enjoy the quiet. I've been awake for an hour already, but I still feel groggy and the headache I woke up with isn't helping.

It took me some time to make sure what I was seeing was real and not just my active imagination caused by being tired. Careful not to step in the puddle of blood and ink, I made my way around the body and squatted down, resting my fingers on the man's neck to check for a pulse. I wobbled upon feeling his skin and almost fell backward. He was gone. I'd never touched a dead body before. I don't know what I expected but the feeling sent a wave of prickles over my skin. The central air was running, causing the skin to be cool, but it still didn't feel the same as touching another living being. I walked to the front door, giving information to the emergency number. I didn't want to be in the shop with a dead stranger lying on my floor.

I sent a text to Declan while I answered the dispatcher's questions about the deceased. I knew I was disturbing his sleep, but I don't want to be here alone. I had no idea how long it would take the officers to collect evidence and remove the body from my shop, which meant I would have to cancel the appointment that I had scheduled for this afternoon. I'm dreading having to make that call.

Declan and Alex arrived at the same time, both men parking directly in front of the building. Declan looked concerned; Alex looked annoyed. I immediately fell into Declan's arms. My being accused of murder was one thing, but finding a dead body is a different level. He wrapped his arms around me but didn't say anything. There was no greeting from Alex. The first thing he asked me was if I touched anything. At first, I just shook my head, but I backtracked. "I touched the body, but only to check for a pulse. I made sure not to step in any of the ink or blood, though."

"I should be thankful for small miracles, I suppose."

"You should give me credit for knowing not to disturb an active crime scene." I could feel my body start to tense up and Alex had only arrived twenty seconds ago.

"Considering this is the second dead body you've been associated with in the past four months, forgive me if I have a hard time giving you credit for anything." He walked past us and into the shop, shining his flashlight in front of him.

I freed myself from Declan's grasp and followed Alex in, Declan was right behind me. "I guess I'm not working today."

Noticing Alex ignored my question, Declan answered for him. "No, probably not." He stepped around me so he could see my face. "Are you okay?"

"Yeah, I'm good. It's just, you know, seeing a body you weren't prepared to see can ruin your day a bit. And, touching it...I wasn't expecting it to feel like that. I don't know what I expected, but..." A shiver ran through my body.

"Let's see if Alex needs anything from us. If not, I need some coffee. It might do you some good to get out of here for a few minutes."

Declan was up later than I was, acting as a moderator of sorts, making sure no one destroyed anything. A few of the guys can get a bit out of control, especially after a few drinks. They never do anything maliciously; the alcohol just makes them careless. I glanced at him and noticed for the first time his eyes were glossy and pink. I felt bad having hi come out so early but he's the only one who can calm me down and relieve any stress I'm feeling simply by his presence. After checking with Alex who told me I only needed to come back to give my statement, Declan and I left the shop and walked across the street.

We got our coffees and walked to the side of the building where I park, making ourselves comfortable on the sidewalk. "I feel so bad having to cancel this appointment. It took us almost four days to agree on a date. I was originally supposed to be on vacation this whole week. I gave up and agreed to the date because it was the only time we could both do it. I scheduled the appointment months ago."

"At least you get the full week now, right?" He always tried to make me feel better. "Besides, it's not like you're canceling because you have the sniffles or something. You know as well as I do, there's no way Alex is going to let you open the shop today."

"I know. I should be thankful I get to take the day off, but I think, under the circumstances, I'd rather work. Plus, I'm not ready to have that conversation. It's bad enough I have to cancel but having to explain it's because there's a dead body in my shop? I can't see that ending well." By the time we finished our drinks, Alex had yellow crime scene tape stretching across the doorway. A small crowd had gathered outside the shop. A few people had their hands clasped to their face and pressed against the windows to see what was happening inside. I sighed. "And so, it begins…again."

Chapter 2

Once Alex took my statement, he let us leave. I called a few friends to invite them over for an impromptu barbecue. I was going against the town's social etiquette by inviting only those I considered friends. If I had the day off, I wanted to do my best to enjoy it. I knew rumors were most likely already spreading through town and I didn't want to actively bring the gossip into my own backyard.

Most of the food was left over from the night before. Falcon took up his spot in front of the grill, keeping careful watch to ensure the hamburgers, kielbasa, and chicken were all grilled to perfection. The smell of the barbecue sauce carried on the air and my stomach rumbled.

Fiona arrived as we were all lining up beside Falcon to get first pick of his grilling expertise. She yelled my name as soon as she came around the corner of the house. "Dakota? What is going on? I heard a rumor you found a dead guy in your shop. Is it true?"

I didn't mind Fiona asking questions. Unlike most of the locals, her questions were inquisitive and full of concern. The others were assuming and judgmental. "It sure is. At least this time they will have a valid reason to think I did it, which I'm assuming they do, since the guy was in my shop."

"Are you okay? I don't know what I would have done if I walked into the coffee shop and found a dead person. I don't think I would sleep for months."

"Yeah. I'm doing all right. I don't think it's fully hit me yet but I'm lucky I have a great group of friends that will help me get through it."

We filled our plates for our late lunch and had just sat down when Alex walked into my backyard. Falcon, of course, was the first to notice his presence and he got up to greet him. "Detective, long time no see. To what do we owe the pleasure?" Although usually full of energy, Falcon was in rare form this afternoon and all but danced around Alex as he was making his way toward the group.

"I'm just here to see Dakota." He sidestepped around him in an attempt to show he had no interest in talking to him and stopped just outside the circle of chairs we had set up. "Dakota, a minute?"

"Whatever you have to say to her, you can say to us." Clyde didn't like it when people left him out of conversations that could have any information. He always preferred to be in the know about every situation that came about whether it involved him or not.

From the corner of my eye, I saw Declan put his hand up and shake his head, telling Clyde to back off. With my plate still in hand, I stood and walked Alex to the porch so we could have a bit of privacy. "What'd you find out?" I noticed for the first time he was dressed in jeans and an old Poison t-shirt. I had to suppress a smile as I imagined him dancing around his kitchen, singing Unskinny Bop at the top of his lungs. I guessed he was planning on a more relaxing day, not getting woken up to investigate a murder.

"He was a tourist, staying in one of the cabins on the lake. The victim's name is Callum MacDonald, went by Mack. Does that name sound familiar to you at all? A friend, client, part of your little group here?" His lip curled when he nodded his head toward them.

My eyes rolled to the sky. It had become an automatic reaction to almost everything Alex said. "The people in this 'little group' are my friends so those two things are one and the same. And, no, I don't recognize the name." I had never witnessed

Alex talking to anyone aside from those he was questioning and I wondered if he was jealous of people who had friends or if he was simply intimidated by the guys because he knew his status as an officer of the law didn't intimidate them.

"Well, let's see if any of your friends know him." He turned toward the group and I watched him square his shoulders. Not bothering to address them in even a mock friendly manner, he yelled from the patio. "Excuse me gentlemen...and ladies. Does anyone here know a man by the name of Callum Macdonald? Nickname Mack."

Most shook their heads, a few grumbled in the negative. Clyde was the only one who spoke up. "Mack? Yeah, I met a guy who called himself Mack on the way down here. We got into a conversation. He told me he was a jeweler, coming down here for a long weekend. Small world." He took a large bite of his burger, leaving a glob of ketchup and mustard in the corner of his mouth, having no idea how bad he just made himself look.

I covered my face with my hand not holding my plate. He really needed to learn that sometimes less is more.

Alex turned to me with a smug look on his face. "Uh huh." He approached the group and targeted Clyde. "Why don't you and I have a little talk." They only walked about ten feet away and we could all hear their entire conversation. "Where did you meet Mack?"

"I don't know. Some place we stopped at for food. About an hour away."

Alex jotted a few words in his notebook. "And he told you he was coming here, specifically?"

"Yeah. I remember because he said 'maybe I'll see you at the fair' and then he got mad when I asked him if he was a carny." He let out a breathy laugh and even from a short distance, we could all see the amusement in his eyes. "He was real mad. That's when he told me he was a jeweler and was coming for a long weekend. He needed a break, I guess."

"Did you guys all ride down together?"

Clyde nodded.

"And none of your friends met him?"

"I was last in line. Mack came up behind me and we started talking."

Alex glanced around the group and gave Clyde a once over. "Do you find it interesting that you're the only one who met the supposed jeweler and you also happen to be the only one of your friends that's wearing more than one or two pieces of jewelry?"

"I can't help it if they don't have any style. I'm not in charge of them."

"That's not what I asked you. You'll be in town a few more days, yes?"

"We're here all weekend. Dakota's letting us stay at her place."

"Great." We all turned our heads and pretended to concentrate on our plates when Alex faced the group again. "Dakota. I'll need the security footage to your building."

I was dreading him asking for that and I had purposely avoided mentioning anything having to do with security. "That might be a problem."

"What's the problem?"

"Well, a few months ago when I got the cameras, I had them on with alerts if they detected any motion. But after you arrested Dennis, I got sick of a random bird flying by or a raccoon looking for its next meal waking me up. I didn't think I really needed the security anymore, so I turned it off."

"You turned off the alerts?"

I shook my head. "I turned off the cameras." I heard Declan grumble beside me and I immediately knew it would be a conversation later.

After Alex left, we all relaxed back into casual conversation. "Dakota, how did your client deal with you having to cancel?" I realized a couple of months ago I didn't actually have to keep an appointment book anymore. Fiona remembered everything that came out of my mouth, including when I had tattoo appointments scheduled. She knew my schedule better than I did.

"As you can imagine, he wasn't happy about it. It took us so long to schedule and we scheduled months in advance so he could take the time off to drive out here. I had the entire day blocked out for him and he already approved the sketch I sent, which took me hours to do. I feel so bad." I always hated having to cancel or even reschedule a client, but this one upset me more than most. My client was coming in for a memorial tattoo for his brother. He lost him while they were both stationed overseas in the army and he requested a color realistic eagle, American flag, and his brother's dog tags. I was honored that he sought me out to tattoo him and I felt awful letting him down.

Falcon was on what I was sure was his third burger. He popped the last bite into his mouth. "Have you considered opening the shop? For quick tattoos, I mean. I bet a lot of people would love to go inside now that it's a murder scene." Fiona hit his leg with the back of her hand. "What? People love stuff like that."

I shook my head. "I didn't even want to go in for the client I had scheduled. Don't get me wrong, I very much wanted to do this tattoo, I just didn't want to do it this week. I'm booked out months in advance and I purposely left this weekend open."

Nikki, who had been almost silent since she arrived, finally spoke up. "I actually think Falcon might be on to something. You could make a lot of money with how many people are in town right now." As usual, she was overdressed for the occasion and the weather. While the rest of us were wearing shorts or jeans and sneakers, she still wore heeled boots, jeans, and a drape-neck polyester top with a thin leather jacket. "Plus, remember last time? I know you'd probably rather forget about it, but you were able to solve Maggie's murder because of a client you had."

"Yes, and he tried to kill me." Before I could finish my response, I heard a knock on the front door. I left the back door open with only the screen door remaining closed, so the sound carried through the house. I wondered who it could be since all my friends were currently sitting in my backyard. A second knock came as I entered the kitchen. "I'm coming." I swung the door open to see Annette trying to catch a glimpse inside through the living room window. In hindsight, I should have left it boarded up after someone threw a rock through it to keep nosy neighbors, like Annette, in suspense. "Can I help you?"

Startled, she turned her head toward me. "Oh, I didn't think you were home."

I raised my hand and gestured across my driveway at the amount of motorcycles and cars parked in it. "I guess that's why you decided to start looking in my windows?"

"Well. That's neither here nor there." She flicked her wrist in an attempt to disregard my observation.

I waited for her to either continue or apologize but she did neither. "It's actually a violation of privacy. What do you want, Annette?"

I stood with my arms crossed over my chest, the door propped open by my shoulder.

"I heard what happened this morning. I came to ask you if you could ask your friends to leave."

I had to give myself a second to force down the laugh that was threatening to escape. "Excuse me?" I didn't almost laugh because it was funny, I wanted to laugh at the absurdity of her suggestion. I couldn't believe she was seriously asking me to make my friends leave.

"You know we hadn't had a murder in this town in many years. A few months ago, when your friends showed up, we had the first and they showed up again yesterday and another murder has taken place. I'm simply not comfortable having your friends here."

This time I didn't stifle the laugh and it came out loud and strong. "In case you've forgotten, they caught the last murderer, who coincidentally happens to be *your* brother. And Declan, who is one of my friends that you're complaining about, is the one who rescued you from your brother's basement and it was his cat who pulled your license from your brother's house to tell us you were there. I can't believe you have the audacity to ask me to tell my friends to leave when your own sibling is a murderer." I spat the last word at her and she gasped.

"Just because they weren't responsible for the first one doesn't mean they aren't responsible for this one."

"My friends could never be responsible for murdering someone. Do you have any idea what kind of people I hang out with, do you know anything about any of them aside from what they look like?"

"No, why would I?"

I felt the heat rise to my cheeks and my heart rate sped up. "Because if you'd take the time to talk to them for a minute instead of judging them, you'd probably realize that they're some of the best people you've ever met." I raised my voice, unintentionally. "Do you know one of the guys sitting back there right now donates a portion of his paycheck, every week, to a children's shelter? One of them volunteers twice a month at a home for adults with special needs. As a group, they run a toy drive every Christmas. And one of them fosters pets for his local pet rescue. Between them, they probably show more humanity in one month than you have in your entire life. Now I'm going to ask you nicely, once, to get off my property. The next time you show up, I'll ask Alex for a restraining order against you."

She huffed and walked down the front steps, calling back over her shoulder. "It says something that you're on a first name basis with the detective."

I slammed the door shut.

"Hey? Are you okay? It sounded like you were yelling a minute ago."

I didn't hear him come in but I was glad he did. Just the sight of Declan made me relax and a rush of relief passed over me. "Yeah, I'm good. I may have raised my voice a little."

"Do you want to tell me what happened?"

"No." I walked past him and swung back around once I entered the kitchen. "That was Annette. She's so lucky I'm not a violent person. Right before she left I threatened her with a restraining order if she comes back. She's just a rotten person, straight down to her core, and she brings out the absolute worst in me."

Declan looked at me with his crooked smile on his face, amused at how fast I changed from not wanting to talk to spewing all of my gripes about Annette. Declan wrapped his arms around me and pulled me close to him. "Do you think I should have let her starve in her brother's basement?"

I was close to tears and his question made me laugh because I was so on edge. "I probably wouldn't argue if you went and put her back."

He released his grip and held me at arm's length. He used his thumb to wipe away the solitary tear that had managed to escape. "Are you sure you're okay? In all the years I've known you, I've never seen you like this."

I shrugged. "I'm fine. I just...you know not many things bother me but sometimes, when a lot happens all at once, it can become a little too overwhelming. I think having Annette show up was enough to push me over. That woman knows how to push every one of my buttons. I've just been a little out of sorts since this morning, but I was trying to ignore it. I'll be fine in a minute."

He leaned forward and kissed my forehead. "You know you can talk to me, right?"

"I know." I smiled, but it was weak. "Thank you." The look in his eyes made me want to fold myself back into his arms and forget everything else around me.

He leaned to the side to look out the screen door that overlooked the back yard. "I don't really want to add anything else to your plate, but when I came in, Falcon was trying to impress Fiona by blowing flame tornadoes from his mouth and I don't really want him getting arrested for accidental arson."

"Impress her? Why? They're already dating." From her observations, Falcon and Fiona seemed to bring out the best in each other.

"You know him. He never was much good when it came to women. He has no idea what to do now that they've been together for a few months. It would be funny if it weren't so sad."

My heart leaped in my chest and I gasped when I reached the back door. Declan slammed into my back and I heard him gasp too. He must have had the same initial thought. It took me a second to realize the flames I saw were from a bonfire they had lit and not from Falcon setting fire to one of the lawn chairs. Laughing, I looked over my shoulder at Declan. "If one of these murderers doesn't kill me, one of our friends might."

Chapter 3

The fourth of July was the town's biggest celebration of the year. They took advantage of the tourist season to maximize profits. They completely fenced off the green and offered admission tickets as weekend passes and day passes. All the local businesses rented tent space and closed their shops for the weekend. When I first heard that, I thought it was a poor business decision. My love of carnivals and fairs started here when I was young, but at the time, I didn't think about the business aspect of things. After seeing how long the line was at the entrance, I changed my mind about the shops closing. The grounds didn't open until nine and I thought I had a great idea with arriving thirty minutes early to beat the crowd.

I should have known better. If I had to guess, I would say the lines started forming around six. It was like black Friday with people lining up to get their big screen TVs and air fryers. I was hoping we'd be able to walk around for a while before it got too busy. Since I was young, I have always loved fairs. I enjoyed the lights and sounds and the smell of fried foods that no one should ever have thought of frying. My stomach rumbled thinking about all the food I planned to consume. Aside from the local businesses, the fair also brought in vendors from nearby states for the typical fair foods. If I didn't know better, I would swear I could already smell the noxious oil mixed with the sweet, sugary stench of fried dough.

Diesel was growing bored with the lack of stimulation and kept crossing between my shoulder and Declan's, trying to find a comfortable place to lie. Instead of his usual leather vest, Diesel wore a long-sleeved T-shirt with Grumpy Bear on the back and a wide brimmed hat to protect his skin from the sun. Sphynx cats are sensitive to the sun's rays due to their lack of fur. Declan hated that I bought his cat a shirt with a Care Bear on it but when I gave him the option of the shirt or a member's only jacket, the angry cartoon won.

Declan shifted his weight from one foot to the other. I knew he was trying not to be obvious, but he hated waiting in line. He looked at me and rolled his eyes. "Why are so many people here this morning? Do they not have anything better to do?"

I shrugged. "Not really. Most of these people are tourists. They're on vacation. Besides, we got here a half hour early, we were going to be standing here this long anyway."

"Yeah, but I didn't expect to have to wait behind two hundred other people."

"I didn't either. I definitely would have had more coffee if I'd known."

Mitzi walked up behind Declan and pushed her head under his arm like a pet would do to get its owner's attention. "What have I missed?"

Declan's lips pinched together and his eyes rolled skyward. "Not much unless you're a fan of standing in line."

I tried to suppress a grin as I watched Declan shift his body in an unsuccessful effort to rid himself of Mitzi without being rude. She had planned ahead and had his wrist in a firm grasp with both her hands, effectively stopping him from removing his arm. They had only met that one time, on my back porch, when she had danced the line of both verbal and physical harassment toward him. "Hey, Mitzi? People won't question you; I have an idea. Can you walk to the front of the line and see what the hold-up is? They were supposed to open twenty minutes ago and we haven't moved at all yet."

"I can do that." She twisted her head, craning her neck as much as she could to look Declan in the face. "What do you say, Casanova?

Arrowsmith

Want to come play detective with me?" Her eyebrows shot up and she winked at him.

"Oh, I'm not comfortable leaving Dakota by herself. I'm sure you heard there was a break-in at her shop."

Mitzi straightened her body in a surprising show of strength, knocking Declan's arm off her shoulder. "I wasn't going to say anything, but you really need to find a way to distance yourself from these events. It's not a good look. Plus, I'm not going to be around forever to give you advice. Another twenty or thirty years and you're going to be on your own." She shrugged and took her leave, making her way toward the front of the line.

"Twenty or thirty years?"

The amusement in Declan's tone made me laugh. "She's determined, I'll give her that, but she's also a bit delusional."

"She called me 'Casanova'."

"Yeah. I don't think she really understands what that means."

"I'm just going to assume she meant she finds me irresistible. Who can blame her? Either way, I guess you don't need me around anymore. Clearly Mitzi will be much better at keeping you safe even though she's like a hundred years old and barely stands higher than my waist."

"I think I'll take my chances with you."

"At your own risk."

It took another forty minutes before we gained access to the fair. According to rumors flying around, half the grounds, including all the games, rides, and main stage, didn't have any electricity even though it had been tested the night before. I didn't care much about whether the rides worked or not aside from enjoying the lights and sounds that came from them. The stage was my concern. The town used a lot of its resources to secure entertainment for the weekend, including music, and almost all the entertainers needed access to the stage.

Declan and I made a quick circle around to see where everything was located before committing to stopping at any booths. I was always amazed at the transformation the green went through at fair time. Having tents, booths, and stanchions everywhere made it look like a completely different space. I also had to wonder how they ever got the area back to its original condition. In the amount of time it took us to make one lap, it was clear to me that no one knew how a trash can worked. Used napkins were already floating by our feet and plates and food wrappers lined the ground around the metal, slotted cans. Bees were beginning to hover, trying to get at the syrup and sweetness of soda that had splashed around the rim.

"I'm thinking about putting up a small flower bed for some honeybees. Maybe toward the edge of my property in the front yard."

"That is a terrible idea." He didn't even glance in my direction.

"I don't know why you can't just be honest with me about how you feel."

His mouth curled up at one corner. "What? It's a bad idea. I hate bees, I'm allergic."

"You're allergic to everything."

"Point is, I hate bees. And with the way things are going, some random person is going to be out on a walk, one of your bees will sting them, and you'll end up with a dead body on your front lawn."

"Wow. Really? Thank you for that boost of confidence, it's exactly what I needed." I turned and started to walk away but he pulled me back and spun me around to face him.

"I didn't mean it like that. You've had a string of bad luck since you moved out here and I think it would be smart if you didn't do anything that could end in disaster." He still had his hands on my waist and I could see in his eyes that he meant what he said with the best intentions.

"Yeah, well. I may do it anyway, just on principal because no one should be in my yard without me inviting them." I reached up and plucked Diesel off his shoulder, cradling him in my arms, and walked away.

"Hey. You can't just steal my cat every time you get mad at me."

I lifted Diesel above my head. "I can and I did." This time it was me who didn't bother to glance back at him. I wasn't mad at Declan; his honesty was one of his best character traits. I was

Calculated in Color

annoyed that he was right. I did want to set up a little garden, but the way things had been going for me the last four months, it wasn't in my best interest to do so. Winter would be here before I knew it anyway so maybe I would wait it out to see if it was something I could do in the spring.

I found myself near the back of the green, the side closest to the rec center and library. Diesel mewled and wriggled out of my arms, dropping to the ground before sprinting around the back of the teacup ride. "Diesel. Get back here." I followed him around the corner and squeezed between two pieces of a metal gate that didn't quite fit together. The amount of cords and wires running from the back of the ride was absurd and I had to keep my head down to make sure I didn't trip. It was no wonder they were having electrical issues this morning.

Diesel was at the far end of the ride, clawing at the largest surge protector I've ever seen. "Hey. Stop that." I bent at the knees to get a better view of what he was pawing at. Right before his paw covered it, I spotted what looked like a green stone in the only outlet not in use. I felt my heart skip a beat as I watched one of his lengthy claws dip into the opening. He pulled the object out and unstuck it from his claw with his teeth. I opened my hand and he dropped the item in my palm. It was a green stone inlaid in a piece of metal. I rolled it around to see that it looked like the button of a shirt. Usually when I see fancier buttons, they're either a clear crystal or mother of pearl. Whoever owned this button, I had no doubt, wouldn't be hard to spot.

"Dakota? What are you doing back there?"

I looked up to see Fiona, Declan, and Falcon standing on the other side of the gate. I closed my fist, so I didn't drop the button and scooped Diesel into my arms. "I thought I'd take a detour." I handed Diesel off to Declan over the gate and worked my way through the opening again.

"What's in your hand?"

"This is from your cat showing off his sleuthing skills again. He pulled it from an outlet over there."

"You let him stick his paw in an outlet?"

"You're infuriating this morning. I didn't let him do it. I told him to stop but he got there a lot quicker than I did after he jumped out of my arms. Maybe you should have trained him better."

He laughed and leaned forward to take a closer look at the button. "You know as well as I do, you can't train a cat. Do you think this was part of the problem with the rides this morning?"

"That's what I was thinking. It wasn't stuck inside or anything, it was kind of laying on top, but I haven't seen anyone working here that would have such fancy buttons on their shirt. Of course, it could have just been stuck to the bottom of someone's shoe."

"At least it's out of the way now. If it did cause any trouble, it won't happen again."

I agreed and dropped the button in my pocket, ready to move on from the topic. "Did you find a place you wanted to grab something to eat? I'm starving."

I don't know how they managed it, but an eating area had been set up in the middle of the grounds with about twenty picnic tables. Fiona and Falcon took their leave again and Declan and I had found an empty table near the edge of the picnic area to sit down after deciding on fried vegetable platters. Wyatt joined us with an overflowing plate of what I could only assume was canned dog food. I watched Declan's lip curl up when the plate hit the table and bits of meat spilled over the side.

"What is that?"

Wyatt's eyes grew wide. "It's a spicy nacho chili dog."

"It looks like dog vomit. And where, exactly, is the dog?"

"It's in here somewhere." Wyatt stabbed at his plate trying to find the hotdog.

Diesel walked across the table and scarfed up the bits that fell off the plate. Declan looked at me and shook his head. "Remind me that I don't want to try that."

"I don't know, Diesel seems to like it."

"Diesel would eat paste if we let him."

"He looks like he already has." Mitzi had appeared out of nowhere and took a seat almost on

Declan's lap. "Have you seen these funnel cakes? It's a good thing I don't have to worry about my figure anymore." She shoveled a fork full of ice cream, chocolate sauce, strawberries, and fried bread into her mouth.

"That's what you're eating for lunch?" I couldn't imagine having a plate of pure sugar for a meal.

"I've got dairy, grains, and fruit. Dessert or not, it hasn't killed me yet." With every bite she took her eyes got larger. The huge, round glasses on her face made it even more obvious.

Nick and Clyde joined us along with a man I didn't recognize and one I wouldn't expect the guys to befriend. He looked like a cross between a surfer and a golfer. His khaki shorts were perfectly pressed and the Hawaiian shirt he wore, covered in pineapples and hibiscus flowers, was bright enough make me squint. He laid his hands on the table for balance as he sat and the sun cast a beam of light off the signet ring on his pinky.

"Hi. I'm Dakota. I don't believe we've met yet."

"Elliott. I've heard a lot about you." His mouth fell open when he saw the look on my face. "Ah, it wasn't all bad. But I just moved in a month ago. I don't remember his name but the guy that attacked you in your shop? I bought his house. I'm sure you know I heard the whole story a number of times."

Calculated in Color

I had heard Celeste sold Dennis' house for next to nothing. Rumor had it he had to sell it to pay for all his court fees. "Of course you did, people love gossip in this town. They can't seem to get enough of it. So, what brought you out here?" I didn't need the answer, I just wanted the conversation to steer away from me.

"Divorce."

"I'm sorry to hear that."

"Oh, I'm not. It was a long time coming. I figured since so much was changing, I would do my best to get a completely fresh start, so I moved from a large city on the west coast to a small town on the east coast. The difference is drastic, but I love it so far. What about you? I heard you're a relatively new resident as well."

"Same thing, except the divorce part. I lived in the city and decided I wanted a slower pace and quieter life." My life has been anything but quiet since I moved out here. "Is it safe to assume you came from California?" I tugged at the strap of my tank top to indicate I was referring to his shirt.

Elliott laughed. "Is it that obvious? My wife hated these shirts. She told me I looked like I belonged on a boardwalk in Miami Beach, so, naturally I bought every one I could find."

"I suppose that does make sense if you're actively trying to *not* work on your marriage." I meant it to be funny, but my tone didn't convey that same message.

He glared at me for a moment before his facial expression softened and he smiled. "Remind me to be careful about what I say around you."

Diesel, who had been sleeping in my lap, picked that moment to raise his paw above the table in an attempt to pull a piece of fried zucchini off my plate. The smile faded from Elliott's face as he watched Diesel's webbed paw attack my plate, and his hand moved slowly over his heart. "What is *that* thing?"

Before Declan or I could answer, Mitzi inserted herself into the conversation. "That's what I've been asking for months. They keep telling me it's a cat. I think it's in desperate need of meeting an iron." She paused and looked around the table. "Before anyone says anything smart, I'm old. I'm supposed to be wrinkly."

Diesel poked his head above the table and glared at Elliott, a low growl coming from deep in his throat. Elliott recoiled at the sound. I scratched the top of Diesel's head, hoping it would calm him. His growl subsided but he kept his eyes narrowed and his ears back. To change the subject for the second time I had to find something else to talk about. "That's a nice ring. It looks vintage."

Elliott looked down at his hand. "Thank you. It was my grandfather's. I don't know what the lion is supposed to indicate but I was fascinated by it as a child. He left it to me when he passed." The whole time he spoke he shifted his gaze from me to Diesel and back again.

"That was certainly nice of him. It's like a small piece of him you get to carry around with you."

He nodded and an awkward silence fell over the table. I felt Declan kick me under the table. "Declan? What do you say you and I go see if we can track down Fiona and Falcon? I told them we would catch up with them as soon as we were done eating." It took no time at all for him to agree and we said our goodbyes to everyone. "He was a little weird, huh?"

Declan shrugged. "He was nice enough, just…a little more reserved than we all are."

"I don't think I trust him."

He paused and looked at me. "You don't trust anyone."

Chapter 4

Alex called my phone to tell me I could access the shop and was nice enough to give me warning about how much there was to clean up. They had a professional team come in for the hazmat stuff, but I was on my own for the rest. It wasn't what I was planning to do today but I wanted to get it over with. Declan texted the guys while I was talking to Alex and all of us rode over to the shop, except Clyde, who brought Diesel back to my house first.

Alex, wherever he happened to be, must have heard us ride by because he showed up at the shop almost immediately after we arrived. "Where's Clyde?"

I wanted to comment on his extreme lack of social skills but decided against it. "He's dropping

Diesel off and then he'll be over. What do you want him for?"

"That's not of your concern."

I rolled my eyes. He's so rude. "Well, did you find out anything more about the guy who died in my shop? Like how he got in or who followed him in or..."

I heard Declan raise his voice. "Don't just put them on the cabinet. These bottles have all been on the floor. You need to pick them up and sanitize them. The whole bottle, before you put them up. Anything and everything needs to be completely wiped down before anything else touches it." His voice was fading in and out between people moving stuff around and the air conditioner rumbling overhead. "Well, you can deal with me or you can deal with Dakota. Your choice."

I felt a pang of appreciation in my heart for how stern he was being. I knew he appreciated the help as much as I did but it wasn't a quick task of simply picking stuff up from the floor. I took a lot of pride in having a clean, sanitary shop and he knew that. He knew I wouldn't have it any other way. "So, any news?"

"Oh, are you talking to me again? I thought you were busy listening to your boyfriend run your business."

"He's not my boyfriend, he just knows how I am. Besides, you should be thankful to know I'm running a legitimate business. Are you going to answer my question?"

"I didn't find out much so far. I went to Mack's room and found a decent amount of jewels and watches. It looks like maybe they were supposed to be for the auction but those had to be turned in three days ago. He should have shipped them rather than bringing them with him."

"Maybe he didn't read the fine print."

"He also didn't have anything registered for the auction. That information was supposed to be submitted months ago."

"He did tell Clyde he was traveling. Those items could be for another place."

"Or they could have been stolen."

I thought about it for a minute. "You think someone killed him over some stolen items? Wouldn't they have collected the pieces as soon as they did it so they could get away before you went looking through his stuff?"

"You make it sound like I was snooping. It's part of my job. They probably killed him before they knew where the items were."

"Serves them right, then. Now they've murdered someone and still don't have the items." As soon as I finished my sentence, Clyde walked through the door.

"Just the guy I was looking for. Let's chat."

They walked no more than five feet away from where I was standing, not that they had a choice, my shop wasn't that big. I took the opportunity to eavesdrop and stayed where I was to listen in.

"You told me you only met Mack on your way down here."

"Yeah."

"Care to tell me why your number is in his phone?"

Clyde was always ready to fight and I watched his body tense and his jaw tighten. "It was in there because I gave it to him. Since we were coming to the same place, I told him to call me if he wanted to get a drink. He seemed like a cool guy."

"You expect me to believe this is all just coincidence?"

"Check his phone. You won't find a single call or text from him. I never heard from him. Seems like someone killed him almost as soon as he got into town."

"I am checking those things. His phone is with our tech team and they'll be able to see all the messages and calls even if he deleted them from his phone."

"Then why are you here?"

Alex turned and walked out the door without saying another word. It was another bad habit he had acquired that I wish he would break.

"Why do you hang out with him?"

I opened my mouth to speak but nothing came out at first. He couldn't be serious. "I don't hang out with him." I wanted to laugh at how absurd his question was. "I don't have a choice when he's investigating a murder that I'm a part of, whether I want to be or not."

Between all of us, it took over four hours to completely clean the shop. We wiped the walls, the chairs, the cabinets, and counters. We swept and mopped the floor in the front and back of the shop. We tasked Joe with sweeping the back and when he swept under a cabinet, he called out to us. He held a green object in his hand. "Have you taken up bead work in your spare time?"

I put my hand out and he dropped the item into my palm. "I don't think this is a bead. It looks like an emerald."

"I've never seen an emerald like that before."

"No. You've probably only ever seen one after it's been cut and polished."

"It looks like moldy plastic."

I shook my head. "I can assure you, it's not." I didn't have any bags, so I wrapped it in a tissue and dropped it in my pocket. "We should stop by the station with this before we head back to the fair."

Declan nodded in agreement.

Before heading back to the fair, Declan and I stopped at the station and I was both relieved and a little upset that Alex wasn't there. I was looking forward to telling him, face to face, that his forensic team didn't do a great job while they were at the shop. The stone was something they never should have missed. I left it with the front desk clerk, along with my contact information and a short statement saying exactly where the item was found.

In all the years we stayed here when I was young, my parents never wanted to attend the auction. As a child, I didn't have any interest in it either, but now, as an adult, I am interested in seeing it. I find it fascinating to see what other people spend their money on. We got there just in time for it to start.

For being such a small town, I was surprised by all the items they had to auction off. The fair committee asked for 'donations' but everyone involved made some sort of profit. The person who owned the items got sixty percent of what the item sold for. My understanding was the town got twenty percent, the auction house they hired also got twenty, and the remaining sixty went to the person who originally owned the item. I thought the auction house would take more of a cut, but I really didn't know anything about auctions. We stood toward the back of the area designated for the auction since we weren't planning on bidding on anything. The crowd was much larger than I would have thought and I wondered if it was the eclectic mix of items being offered or if that many people were really interested in the auction process. I'm sure there were some, like me, who just wanted to see the process but that would only account for a small number. The town planned well and had a projector set up so people further back would be able to see the items on the large screen behind the stage. Fiona told me they had one hour earlier in the day to get a closer look at the items to decide if and what they wanted to bid on.

When I first heard about the auction, I thought it was more of a silent auction where people would bid on fancy gift baskets, maybe a trip somewhere. I imagined it would be all the local shops and maybe some of the vendors that put together some items for donation. I didn't realize half the tourists came around specifically for this purpose. They had sports memorabilia, artwork, furniture, jewelry, and even a couple of rare coins. The auctioneers divided it nicely and instead of auctioning all the coins back-to-back, they chose one item from each category to keep everyone interested. I thought some of the items were boring but watching the excitement of the people who were interested in them was fun. In total, it took just over three hours for all the items to sell and by the time it finished, I was ready for bed. I asked Declan if he would bring me home, expecting him to come back out. We went back to my house, but he didn't leave. Both of us were fast asleep within twenty minutes.

Chapter 5

It was only two days ago that Falcon suggested I open the shop to have firsthand access to what people were saying about the murder. I considered it briefly and decided against it. I had purposely not scheduled any appointments during these few days because I wanted to enjoy the holiday. I also wanted to make up for not spending time with all my friends the first time they all came out here during my grand opening weekend. The coffee shop was still open for three hours in the morning before the fair started for the day and I needed something stronger than just the regular coffee I made at home.

    I left the guys to fend for themselves. I grabbed my bag, leaned down so Diesel could crawl on my shoulder, and drove toward the shop with the cat still perched on my shoulder like a parrot. "Oh, you've got to be kidding me." I slowed down to survey the scene that was taking place before me. I thought I left early enough that most residents and tourists would still be sleeping, or at least taking their time before going out. I was wrong. There was a whole crowd of people standing outside the shop. Fortunately, it wasn't the coffee shop. Unfortunately, it was my shop.

Thankful that I drove up the back side of the coffee shop, I crept along to see if I could figure out what was happening. The sun was barely up and the air still had a slight chill to it but that didn't seem to stop those with inquiring minds. My heart pounded and my anxiety grew as I imagined all different scenarios for why everyone would be outside. Was there another body? Were they all waiting for me to show up so they could harass me about being a suspect again? Thankful I had thrown a hoodie on, I pulled the hood over my head, dumped the contents of my bag on the floor of my Jeep, and let Diesel crawl inside so we wouldn't be quite so obvious. I made a mad dash toward the coffee shop, hoping no one would recognize me.

As soon as I walked in, I saw Fiona's eyes grow wide and she made her way around the counter. "I'm so glad you're here. I've been trying to send you a message for twenty minutes, but the line hasn't stopped. Did you see all those people outside?"

"They're hard to miss. What is going on?"

She shook her head in a way that told me I wasn't going to like the answer. "They want you to open the shop. I think it's that, what do you call it, morbid curiosity? If I were you, I'd take it and run. Let them pay you just to see where a murder took place." Her mouth fell open and she pulled in a sharp breath. "I didn't mean..."

I had to laugh. Putting her foot in her mouth due to her lack of thinking before she spoke was one of her most endearing qualities, even when it was at my expense. "I know what you meant, it's okay. Falcon suggested it a couple of days ago and I considered it but decided against it. Maybe I should open, even if it's only for a couple of hours." I waited while she made my coffee, running different options through my head. Maybe I will open the shop, if I can get some sort of security detail to stay outside.

My original plan, since I had already left the house, was to go to the shop to work on a design for a client that's coming in next week. Diesel would have been perfectly happy to curl up on the bench outside, basking in the sun for an hour or two. There was no way I was going to try to wrestle my way through the crowd, so I drove back home instead. I found Declan sitting at the kitchen table, coffee mug in hand. "Morning."

He looked up at me and I could tell he still wasn't fully awake. His eyes went from my face, to my coffee cup, to Diesel, who was still sitting on my shoulder. "Good morning. Nice to see you didn't bring me coffee and you kidnapped my cat." One corner of his mouth turned up in a smirk.

"I wasn't planning on coming back so soon." I sank into the chair opposite him and Diesel walked across the table to him. "We have a problem." Declan's eyebrows shot up and he waited for me to continue. My eyes focused past his head to the yellow paint I put on the kitchen walls. I read somewhere that having a sunny color in the kitchen could improve one's mood, so I decided to try it since I finally owned my own space. Sometimes it was nice, other times it felt overwhelming, like it was trying to force a mood I wasn't feeling. This is one of those times. "People are outside my shop, practically protesting for me to open."

"Protesting?"

"Practically protesting. They don't have signs or anything but there's a huge crowd standing outside. Fiona thinks they want me to open so they can satisfy their morbid curiosity." My eyes locked on his and he slowly shook his head. I knew he was putting up his own protest before I could even ask him, but I didn't let it stop me. "I think I might do it, just for a few hours this afternoon. I'll throw together some flash pieces, make them fair-esque, cotton candy, ice cream, that sort of thing. But...I feel like I would need to have some sort of security at the door that only allows a couple of clients at a time, and I was thinking maybe you could help me for a while."

His facial expression hadn't changed since I started talking, it was showing no emotion at all. "You want me to be a bodyguard? A bouncer?"

"Well, no." I put on the sweetest smile I could. "I was hoping maybe a couple of the guys would volunteer. You know Clyde is always looking for confrontation, so I don't think I'd have to ask him twice. I thought maybe you'd be willing to do a few tattoos so you could be inside with me." I formed it as a statement rather than a question, hoping he'd pick up on it.

"Dakota. We talked about this. I haven't tattooed in years. It's not that I haven't thought about it, I'm just not sure I want to go back to it."

"But this can help you decide. I'm not asking you to commit to tattooing full time, just a few hours this afternoon to satisfy all the curious tourists. A couple of hours won't hurt. Besides, tattooing is like riding a bike, once you pick up a machine, it'll be like you never stopped."

He stared at the table and shifted his mug back and forth across the surface, sighing. "I don't even have any machines. I put them all in storage."

"And you think I only have one?" A low grumble made its way up his throat and I knew I had him. I did my best to suppress a smile.

"Fine." The word came out through clenched teeth, but I knew him better than that. He would do anything to help me and I was confident once he picked up a machine, he would remember how much he loved it and these few hours might be enough to convince him to go back to it.

Before he had a chance to change his mind, I ran to the bedroom and grabbed his tablet, pulled my own out of my bag, and sat back at the table. "Let's get our fair flash on."

Declan tried not to laugh. "If you make a comment like that again, I'm quitting."

"You know you loved it."

We spent the next two hours drawing pieces we thought we could use while the guys trickled in looking for food and coffee. "Can you imagine sleeping until nine or nine-thirty?"

"I don't remember the last time I slept until seven." Declan spun his tablet around so I could see what he had accomplished. Between the two of us, we had come up with a pink teddy bear, a crude rendering of a ferris wheel, an upside-down ice cream cone, a dancing chili-dog, a green balloon poodle, a clown face, and a few others.

"You couldn't have left the clowns out, huh?" He knew I hated clowns. I've hated them since I was young. "I'm not doing that one."

"It's a classic fair icon."

"Nope. You can do those."

We convinced Clyde and Wyatt to stand guard outside the shop. Fiona was right about opening. It wouldn't hurt to pull in some business and take advantage of the curious minds. None of us were planning to go to the fair until evening anyway. They had a few bands lined up to play and that's what we were all looking forward to. Our plan for the day was simple. Since we didn't have any appointments set up, we would only allow two people in the shop at any given time. Once we finished with one person, we'd allow another to come in. Not knowing who I could trust was a bit of a deterrent to having multiple people come in at once and if we only had two, it would stop people from trying to snoop around while they were there.

Declan and I agreed to open for five hours or until the crowd died down. Part of me hoped by the time we got to the shop, the horde of people would have dispersed so we could relax for the day instead. It didn't. It had grown to what I would guess was three times the size it was when I was here earlier. When we all pulled up, we saw Alex doing his best to control the crowd that had migrated into the street. There wasn't any traffic because most tourists and locals were at the fair but if there were, the crowd would have been blocking it.

Wyatt and Clyde pulled their bikes onto the sidewalk and parked sideways on either side of the door, effectively clearing a path for Declan and I to enter the shop. They also eliminated the mob crowding the door allowing Alex to walk in directly behind us.

"Was this your idea?" He stood with his arms crossed, sweat dripped down his temple. It was only ten in the morning, but it was clear the crowd control took a lot out of him. It was nowhere near hot enough for him to be sweating like that yet.

"No. But I figured I might as well take advantage of it."

"You can't have people blocking the street. They're about to start rioting. This is exactly why people didn't want you here to begin with."

"I'm sorry you've had a tough morning, but this isn't my fault. I didn't ask for any of these people to come here. I was supposed to have these four days off so I could enjoy the fair and spend time with my friends. And to be fair, you didn't look like you were doing a great job controlling the crowd, so how do you expect me to?"

Declan had already gone to the back and wheeled out an extra table and started filling his cart with supplies. "Hey." He nodded his head toward the window. "It looks like they were able to get some sort of order going out there."

"Ha. Or maybe you just needed my friends to do your job for you." When we walked in, Alex was trying to push people who were spilling into the street back onto the sidewalk. Some were standing in haphazard groups along the front of the building, a few loners were standing in the grass and trampling through the flower bushes that flanked the cement benches. Now, the entire

Calculated in Color

crowd had organized, at the insistence of Clyde and Wyatt, into two single file lines, one on each side of the entrance.

Alex rolled his eyes and made his way to the door. "Don't make me come back out here."

"Trust me, if I have any choice, I won't."

The first two hours flew by without incident. We took one client after the next, but the line never seemed to get any shorter. To save time, we left copies of the flash with the two outside so people already knew what they wanted before they came inside. Falcon let my next client in and I greeted him just like I had everyone else prior. "Okay, I just need to see your ID and then I'll need a signature at the bottom of this page."

While most of our clients had toned down their energy before coming in, this gentleman didn't seem to get the memo. He was fidgety and sweating. Round glasses sat on his nose, his hair stood on end like he had been running his fingers through it for hours, and it looked like he hadn't shaved or showered in at least a few days. He ignored my request for his ID and walked around the counter, his eyes growing rounder by the second.

"Whoa. Is this where the body was?" He pulled his glasses down and crouched in front of the back door. He pulled his phone from his pocket and took pictures of the stain on the floor. He pointed to the mark. "This, right here, is amazing. I can't believe I get to see it first-hand."

A cleanup crew had come in to clean and sanitize the shop, but I still had work to do to remove the ink stain from the floor. I hadn't decided yet whether I was going sand it down and re-varnish it or if I was just going to replace the wood in that area. Neither option was a small task. The man stood up and started taking picture after picture, turning in a circle to get a full 360-degree rotation.

"Excuse me. We're not here for a photo op. If you'd like a tattoo, I need to see your ID. Otherwise, the door is that way." I pointed him back up front. From the corner of my eye, I saw Declan glance up at me. He always found it amusing when I so direct with people. I was almost never rude to a client but at this point I wasn't sure if this guy was a client or if he just took the opportunity when he saw it to come into the shop.

"Oh right, right. Sorry. I just got excited when I saw the area because I heard he died right in the doorway to the back room and I wanted to see it for myself." He pulled his license from his wallet and I couldn't help but notice it was nylon with a full velcro strip. He had probably had the same one since he was ten. "I have a podcast about murders and this will be a great addition for this month. You should take down my web address so you can watch it. I'm going to call it 'The Fourth Fair Firefight'."

I heard Declan's machine turn off and I gave him a quick glance. "He wasn't shot."

Calculated in Color

"Oh. No? Hmm...are you sure? Because that's a great title."

"I'm positive. Go ahead and sign here." I slid the consent form across the counter along with a pen.

He signed and then made himself comfortable on the table. "You know I was joking about him being shot, right? I just need to make sure what the locals are saying about a stabbing is true."

"Yeah. It's best to get all your facts straight before you mistakenly spread lies all over the internet." I knew he was fishing for information, but he wasn't going to get it from me. Alex was the only one authorized to talk about details of an investigation and the last thing I needed was him knocking on my door because I said too much to someone.

He nodded his head in agreement. "I knew you'd understand." He was quiet for the next few minutes, tapping his foot on the floor. Even with the radio on, all I could here was his shoe hitting the floor. "So, what's it like being a murder suspect two times? Is it as exciting as I think it would be?" He smiled with his mouth wide open and it gave off chilling vibes.

"Well, this has been fun, but I didn't agree to be interviewed and you're all done." I swiped a towel with witch hazel over the tattooed area of his wrist and couldn't have been happier to see him walk out the door. I didn't make a habit of not finishing a tattoo, especially pieces this small but I didn't trust him. He didn't even look at the tattoo when I told him I finished. He walked out of the shop with a teddy bear with a pink head and body, the arms, legs, and ears, nothing more than an outline.

The rest of the afternoon carried on exactly like that customer. Declan and I found ourselves constantly reeling people back in. After the fourth hour, I realized instead of tattooing, we should have just charged people an admission fee and let them do a walk-through of the shop. When we took the last two clients of the day, we could hear the grumbling from those still left in line and if it weren't for the two of us being completely exhausted, I may have offered people that walk-through tour. Wyatt and Clyde joined us after they dismissed the rest of the line and waited until we finished with our last clients.

Declan shook his arm out as I locked the door. "My hand and wrist are cramping so bad. I guess I was more out of practice than I thought."

"That'll happen when you jump into a five hour stretch after taking years away from your craft. Did you find out anything good from any of your clients?"

He shook his head. "Not a thing. Nothing useful anyway, most of them just wanted to ask questions. Speaking of, what was up with your podcast guy?"

"Oh!" I rolled my eyes and started combing through the consent forms, looking for his. "Jeremy Bivens, twenty-seven, no doubt he lives in his mother's basement. He creeped me out, I sent him away with half a tattoo."

"What?"

"It's fine...it looks complete, I just didn't finish the color. Ah-ha. He left the web address for his podcast under his signature."

"Perfect. Let's give him a couple of hours and we'll check to see if he posts anything about being here today."

Everyone pitched in to help me clean up the shop so we could head over to the fair. It was dinner time, we were all starving, and I had a Sonoran hotdog calling my name. All of us were looking forward to joining the rest of the group and relaxing while enjoying some music.

Chapter 6

There were two bands lined up for the night. The first was a blue grass band. It's not something I would go out of my way to listen to, but I was surprised how easily I fell into the rhythm and was able to appreciate the talent. By way of free entertainment, I wouldn't hesitate to see another. The second one was the one I was excited to see. They performed covers for all different rock bands and while they were on stage, I forgot about everything that was bothering me. It did exactly as I hoped it would.

Leyland had joined us at some point during the show. I waved to him, but it was too loud to have any sort of conversation. We had our differences when I first moved out here and I all but accused him of murdering his ex-girlfriend. In the months since, we realized we had quite a bit in common and he was nothing like the person others warned me about. He left town for a few years after graduating from high school and it seemed that was all he needed to get his life and attitude together. "Hey. I'm sorry I didn't make it to your place the other day. I was out of town."

"Visiting the new Mrs.?"

A broad smile swept across his face. "I was. It sucks that she's so far away, but she told me after grad school so would consider moving out here."

"That's excellent. I'm so happy for you."

"It's been tough. You know, when Maggie and I broke up it hit me hard. And then when I moved back, I was hoping to reconcile with her but we both know that will never happen now. I know it hasn't been that long, but I really didn't think I would ever find someone who would fill that void. Enough about me though, what is happening around here? I just got back yesterday and I've heard all kinds of rumors floating around."

"You know how quick talk gets around this town. The bad part is most of what you heard is probably not rumors. The day I texted you, asking you to stop by, I found a dead body in my shop. It wasn't a great start to my morning."

His face twisted into a grimace. "I wouldn't imagine so. I'm guessing you're a suspect again?"

"So far, Alex hasn't come right out and said it but I'm going with the assumption that I am. I found the guy in my shop so..."

"Dakota? We're all going back to your place to get another bonfire going. Are you coming?" Clyde and Falcon must have appointed Nick to be their messenger.

There was never any question, if Clyde was around, a bonfire was going to happen whether it was snowing outside or the temperature was one-hundred degrees. "Yeah, I'll be right behind you. Don't let Falcon touch the fire." I turned my attention back to Leyland. "You want to come over? I'm sure these guys will still be awake for hours."

"Sure. I probably won't stay long but I'll meet you over there."

Declan and I couldn't have been more than ten minutes behind everyone else but by the time we got back to my house, the party was in full swing. The bonfire was already raging and scattered across my backyard were people I didn't even know. Even though I wasn't thrilled about having random people at my house, I would have been able to tolerate it better if my friends had asked me first. I think my friends forgot there's a murderer running around the town and I've had enough socializing for the day.

We made ourselves comfortable on the back porch, away from the main activity, where I had a good vantage point. Declan pulled out his phone and turned the screen toward me. "It looks like your friend posted a video from earlier today."

"I'm afraid to watch it." I could only assume it had been heavily edited and I wasn't looking forward to seeing what he turned the makeshift interview into. Declan pressed the play button and I held my breath while I waited for it to load.

'Welcome back, guys. I only have a teaser for you so far, but rest assured, the full story will be available soon. Do you ever wonder how I get in on all the action? It's a skill. I go where the leads take me and this weekend, the leads took me to a little podunk town where everyone knows everyone and a local business owner is a suspect in a murder for the second time since she moved to town.' A picture of my face flashed on the screen and I gasped. 'Dakota Maddison, the owner of the town's tattoo shop, Satin Mystique, found the body of Callum MacDonald inside her shop just two days ago. Now, before you ask, the police were able to find the killer in the first murder and it wasn't Dakota. But one has to question whether this is a terrible coincidence or if she's good enough to frame not one, but two people for murders she's committing.'

"That little sh..." I clamped my mouth shut before finishing my sentence. Seeing a picture of my shop on the screen made every muscle in my body tense up. "He may be my first real murder."

Declan gave me half a smile. "Look on the bright side, it's free advertising."

I glared at him before focusing on his phone again.

'...the victim, Callum MacDonald, aka Mack, is a jeweler from northern Idaho. At least, that's what he wants everyone to believe. As I mentioned earlier, I have skills and I know how to use them to my advantage. Mack wasn't the man he claimed to be and I have proof. He came to this little town with a purpose and even though he's not alive anymore to fulfill his mission... I am here and I intend to do it for him.'

"I have no idea what that means."

Declan hit the home button on his phone and set it on the table. "Do you think we should just ask him? You do have his number at the shop."

"I want to. But I don't think it's appropriate to use information from the consent form. Maybe we should ask Alex if we see him and we can keep an eye out for our podcast friend in the meantime."

"And since that won't happen tonight, we should go see what everyone is up to."

I sighed and nodded. I wanted nothing less than to join everyone. It made me happy knowing they were all here, but I wanted to curl up in bed and stay there for a day or two. In the time it took us to watch the video, more people had come to join the party. Nikki and Kerry were in conversation with Mitzi and Temperence. Leyland and Falcon were chatting with someone I had never met and Fiona and Clyde were also conversing with two people I didn't recognize.

Celeste was sitting in a chair next to the fire with a look of terror on her face; Diesel had taken up residence on her lap and she did not look okay with it. "You don't look very happy." I tried to smile to play it off. "Can I take him for you?" I reached down and scooped Diesel up when she nodded.

"I'm not really a cat person even though he seems to be a people cat." She looked relieved by having him removed from her lap.

"He's not. He's a 'who can I make the most uncomfortable' type cat."

"He looks angry."

"It's the wrinkles. They give him a permanent scowl. He's actually really sweet, just has a bit of an attitude." I sat in the chair next to her and Diesel curled up in my lap against my stomach. "How have you been? I feel like it's been a while since we've talked."

"It has and I'm doing well. This time of year is always busy with tourists thinking they may want to move here, people looking for a place to retire. I'm thankful for the time off during the fair, though."

"I heard you finally sold Maggie's house." Being in such a small town, the houses were more than affordable but it was rare that one went on the market and they usually never lasted long.

Celeste sighed. "I did. I was beginning to think I would never sell it. I'm not sure why every buyer wants to know where the previous owner went but all the prospective buyers for her house acted like she suffered a brutal murder *in* the house. No one wanted to touch it. I ended up selling it to a couple who are retiring next year." She turned her head and pointed. "That's the husband over there. His name is Brooks Harmon."

She referred to the person I didn't know talking to Leyland and Falcon. They must have heard us talking about him because they were moving in our direction. As they got closer, I could see his name was fitting. The metal toe plates on his cowboy boots reflected the light from the fire, as did his belt buckle. He wore a tan, button down shirt covered in images of a bucking stallion.

"Brooks, it's nice to see you again. Have you met Dakota yet? This is her house you're at."

"Celeste, always a pleasure. Miss Dakota." He extended his hand to shake mine. "Pleased to make your acquaintance." He took a seat next to me.

"It's nice to meet you. Celeste was just telling me you purchased a house here."

Brooks nodded. "My wife, Diane, and I will be moving here just as soon as I manage to sell the business."

"Oh? What do you do?"

"Now I know I don't look the part, but I'm an antiques dealer and auctioneer. Sold." He yelled the last word and it made us all jump, but we laughed at his quip about not looking the part. "You're friend over here tells me you have your own business. A tattoo parlor?"

"Mhm. I do."

"Shame what happened there. Hope it doesn't impact you too much." He unfastened a cuff link, rolled up his sleeve, and turned his forearm toward me. "Got this beauty while I was serving in the navy."

"Very nice." Unfortunately, after a few decades and what I assume was a significant amount of sun exposure, it looked like he was in rough waters while he was getting it done. "You know, if you wanted, I could fix that up for you a bit. Make it look almost brand new again."

"I appreciate the kind offer, but I'll decline. A dear friend of mine did this anchor and he's no longer with us. This piece will remain as is."

"Well, if you ever change your mind." I looked over and saw Declan talking to Elliott. I wondered if he was getting the same vibes I got from him yesterday. I couldn't quite place it, but there was something off about him, something I didn't trust.

Brooks slid forward in his chair and leaned back to reach into his pocket. He pulled out a pocket watch and clicked open the front. "Time sure is getting on today."

Diesel shifted in my lap and I felt his claws dig into my thigh. "Ow. What is the matter with you?" I unhooked his paws from my leg but could still feel how rigid his body had become.

Brooks scrunched his face. "Oh. He looks like a gargoyle."

Diesel's ears laid flat on his head and his mouth opened just enough to show his front teeth. If he was trying to not look like a gargoyle, he was failing miserably. "Is your watch antique? It's lovely, from what I can see in the firelight, anyway."

"Yes, ma'am. The good part of owning my own store is being able to buy for myself if I find something I like. I have rings, bracelets, watches, a house full of furniture. The downside is the stuff I like best is also the stuff I can sell for the most money, but I can't bear to part with some of it."

"I can see that being a problem. I don't know if I would be able to resist myself. Older pieces of, anything really, have a certain aesthetic and personality to them that make it easy to fall in love."

"They sure do."

Diesel started twisting in my lap again and I used that as a reason to excuse myself. I brought him inside to get his vest thinking maybe the fire wasn't doing a good enough job keeping him warm. I set him on the table and he stood on his hind legs so I could slip the vest around his front legs. He leaned forward and stretched his paws so I would pick him up again. "I'm guessing you're not a big fan of Brooks?" His body was still tense, so I rubbed the back of his neck on our walk back outside to go find Declan.

He turned in my arms when he heard Declan's voice and his low growl started again but quickly turned into him squirming in my arms and hissing.

"Excuse me for a minute." Declan walked away from Elliott and reached out to get control of Diesel. "What did you do to him?"

"Nothing. We were sitting by the fire, having a conversation, and he got really tense, clawed me, and wouldn't relax. I went to get his vest and as soon as we got down here, he started going crazy." I was thankful Declan also had his vest on because Diesel was trying to climb over his shoulder by using his claws for traction. "I don't think he likes either of our two new friends."

"He may have good reason." We had just entered the kitchen and sat at the table. "Remember you were telling me you had a weird feeling about Elliott? During our conversation, he let it slip that he knew Mack."

"The dead guy from my shop? How? Why?"

"It's a good thing you're sitting down. We started talking about what happened at your shop and apparently, he saw a picture of Mack...on some social media page of your podcast friend. I guess he's a big fan. Anyway, he told me he met Mack a few years ago at an antiques show in California."

"Huh."

Declan squinted at me. "That's all you have to say?" He removed Diesel's vest and the cat rolled over on the table asking for belly rubs.

I put one finger up to tell him to give me a minute while I sorted my thoughts. "Okay. So, it

Calculated in Color

makes sense that Mack would be at an antiques show because he's a jeweler. They probably have a ton of items in that category. But in the podcast, that guy said Mack isn't who he appears to be. It's also a little strange, probably coincidence, but the guy I was just talking to said he's an antiques dealer and auctioneer. Do you think they all know each other?"

Chapter 7

Declan came into the bedroom and woke me up. "I made you some breakfast. Hurry and get up before one of the guys eat it."

I stretched and blinked my eyes a few times. "I'm awake. Give me a couple minutes and I'll be out." I threw a hoodie on over my tank top and sat on the edge of the bed. I was still tired, but I thought it was more emotional than anything. I was so comfortable all night. Declan had been sharing my room since there were so many people in my house and at one point, I woke up to find him curled around me. I fell back to sleep almost immediately after shifting my body closer to his and now I couldn't tell whether it was real or if I was dreaming. Either way, it felt good. I shook my head to shake the thought free and went to the kitchen. I sat down just in time to see Declan give Diesel his plate of bacon and I felt a small twinge of...something. I had watched him do it so many times before and it shouldn't bother me either way; he was feeding a cat. There was nothing significant in the action.

"How'd you sleep?"

The question caught me off guard and the thoughts of his arm wrapped around me came flooding back. "Fine." The word came out so fast it didn't even convince me. "You?" *What was this?* Any other time I would have found something more interesting to say or I would have guessed how he slept by how early he was awake or whether his hair was sticking up. I've never responded by asking him in return.

I saw his eyes squint just a little before he recovered. "Very well. I was either a lot more tired than I thought or I was extremely comfortable."

My cheeks grew hot and I covered my face with my hands, pretending to rub my eyes.

He set a plate in front of me, along with a cup of coffee before grabbing his own and joining me. "I tried to find that social media page Elliott was telling me about last night, but I can't find it. I thought his podcast would have links to all his other pages, but it doesn't."

"I'm sure you already tried typing in his handle and the name of the podcast to see what else came up?"

He nodded while chewing. "I did. It seems like every page he has is under a different name. It doesn't make much sense if you ask me. Usually, when you have a following, you want to somehow connect all your socials so people can follow you on all your pages. This whole situation seems to get weirder the more we find out." He stood up to get more coffee and my eyes moved up and down his body.

I forced myself to look out the back door and tried to focus on processing what he just told me. "That is weird. All of my handles match. It's the best way for people to find you."

"Exactly." He sat back down and continued eating. "I also listened to a few of his other short podcasts. I didn't find them all that interesting, but he thinks he's amazing."

"Mhm. I got that impression. He seems to think he's a lot smarter than he really is. I found him more annoying than anything."

"While I was waiting for the coffee to brew, I tried to look up past auctions in California. That could take weeks. Do you have any idea how many take place in that state throughout the year?" I shook my head. "A lot. Anyway, I woke you up so you could eat and shower before everyone else starts getting up. You have to be at the fair early today, right?"

"Oh, I almost forgot." Almost two months ago I had signed up to judge the baking competition. I didn't want to do it at first but

Temperance all but begged me, going on about how so few people would be able to try everything with all the allergies everyone had now. The fact that I could eat anything meant I had little choice. "I'm so glad one of us is paying attention to my responsibilities because I'm certainly not."

I finished my breakfast and by the time I showered and dressed, Declan was ready to go and Diesel was already wearing his vest and helmet. He had to be the coolest cat I'd ever met. Over the last four days, I had only seen my own cat darting from one room to the next, doing his best to hide from everyone, including me. After everyone leaves, it'll probably take him another two weeks to forgive me.

I felt like I was going to explode by the time the judging was over. They had four different categories: pies, cakes, cookies, and sweet treats which included everything that didn't fall under the other three. The amount of talent people in this town had was mind blowing. Out of everything I tried, there were only six that I didn't care for at all. Someone made a maple pecan log that was so sweet it didn't even have a taste. I tried a gingersnap cookie that I expected to be hard, but I physically couldn't bite into it; I would have had better luck eating a brick. One pie topped all the other bad items. I didn't even know how to rate it by looks or taste. It was supposed to be apple, but

Calculated in Color

I'm convinced the baker used applesauce instead of apple slices. The texture alone was a turnoff.

The contest was set up so we were to judge blindly. We had no idea who baked what. There were four judges and we all had to rank each entry on a scale of one to five to determine the top three. After we tallied all the votes, unlike other contests I've seen, they announced the winners for each category over a microphone and the winner came up on stage to collect their ribbon. For the first three categories, you could see the disappointment on some faces, but the announcements went smoothly. They saved the pie category for last. It had the highest number of entries and I knew people took their pie baking very seriously.

I watched Annette make her way to the front row for the final three ribbons and I knew immediately that she had submitted an entry. She smiled when they announced third place. It was the first time I ever recall seeing her smile. Her smile grew wider when she didn't hear her name for second place. The first-place ribbon was all that was left and she had a grin so wide it swallowed most of her face. She balled her hands into fists and she could hardly wait to go up and claim the prize. When they called the winner, she stood perfectly still except for her mouth slowly falling open. Almost as if it were in slow motion, she bolted to the stairs that led to the stage, pushed the winner off the bottom step, and came to rest at the top of the stairs.

Arrowsmith

"I demand a recount." She stood with her hands on her hips, her chest rising and falling with deep, quick breaths. "This contest was fixed and it's her fault." She pointed straight at me and her glare followed.

Temperance was the judge who was making the announcements and she turned to look at me. I shrugged. It was all I could do. This was my first time at the fair as an adult, my first time judging this contest. I didn't even know Annette had entered anything. "Annette, please calm down. The contest is not rigged."

"I win every year and I didn't even place. I want the votes recounted."

"Like every year, you can look at the scores once we're done here. We judge blindly but the scores are not confidential."

She pointed at me again. "She's out to get me because I'm the only one brave enough to say what everyone else is thinking. She and her friends are murderers and criminals and I want them all out of our town." Annette huffed and stomped her foot. "I want her fired."

Temperance turned her face away so Annette couldn't see her stifle her laugh. "That's not fair and it's not how all of us feel. That's how you feel. We also can't fire her, she's a volunteer. Now if you'll step to the side, the winner would like to claim her ribbon." As soon as the words were out of her mouth, two security guards ascended the stairs and forced Annette to move.

I didn't stick around to see her look over the voting cards, but I heard after the fact that I scored her pie the highest out of the four judges. Needless to say, she was not happy to see the results.

Chapter 8

Aside from going to the library to check out books every year, the most vivid memory I have of my summers here are the fireworks shows. For the fair, they always do shows on two different nights. Tonight was the first for this year and Fiona met all of us on the bleachers behind the high school. I had never been over this way, but she told me it was the best viewing spot and guaranteed there wouldn't be as many people over that way. She was right. Aside from some high school students, it was just our group and was much quieter than the green.

I leaned into Declan to get his attention. "Hey, I have a question for you."

"Okay."

Arrowsmith

"Have you given any consideration to going back to tattooing?" I was hesitant to ask. He stepped away from it years ago and seemed content working for himself, on his own time, from the comfort of his home or my home or anywhere else he happened to be.

He shook his head and stared at me silently for a moment. "I miss it every once in a while. But then I remember why I left three different shops and why I went into business for myself."

"You never told me why you left."

"Pay. My art is very important to me, regardless of the medium. I was sick of working for people who made more money off it than I did. Why should I have to pay the shop owner almost fifty percent of every tattoo I do and still have to buy my own supplies?"

"Oh, so you mean you because most of them run their shop like every other corporation?" I watched as he nodded his head and then as his face fell when he remembered I also owned my own shop. His mouth opened and I cut him off before he could say anything. "I get it. That's the exact reason I opened my own shop and also why it was such a hard decision for me to close my first one. I know how hard it is to find a shop that pays fairly and I felt awful about leaving the artists who worked in my shop, forcing them to find a new place where they could make the same amount."

"I never asked you, it wasn't my business, but since you brought it up..."

"I did what I wish every shop did. All my artists are independent contractors. I purchase all the supplies and charge my artists a weekly fee for renting the space. They set their own schedules, they can come and go as they please, and how much they charge and make is up to them." Declan was staring at the sky and I wondered if he was actually listening to what I was saying. "I think the way I do things is fair because it forces the artists to go out and pull clients in to make their own paycheck and I knew how much to expect every week, so I knew my lease and shop bills were taken care of for the month."

"I would have loved that. At least your artists know where their money is going every week, rent and supplies. And every client they bring in is helping them pay their own bills rather than lining the owner's pockets."

"Exactly." It was my turn to stare off at the darkened sky. I wanted to ask but didn't want to ask directly and put him in the awkward position to say 'no.' "You know, when I moved out here, I had appointments scheduled months in advance. Enough so I didn't have to worry about paying the rent or my bills, even if I had a couple of cancellations. I left some time open so I could also take walk-ins or schedule some smaller tattoos, but I didn't expect to be as busy as I am. I know it's tourist season and that's where most of the extra people are coming from, but I wonder if I need to bring in another artist, either full time or maybe just for the summers." I refused to look directly at him even though I could feel his eyes on me. I was dreading the possibility that he might outright tell me he wasn't interested.

"That might not be a bad idea considering how busy you've been. If you want my advice, I'd wait to see how the rest of the summer plays out. You still have two months left. Then see what happens over the holidays. If you want more time to yourself or feel like you have enough business to bring in another artist, you can do it after the new year."

His logical thinking over the past couple of days was beginning to get to me. I knew it was a long shot, but I was hoping he would make a rash decision and just offer to stay without me having to ask him. I hesitated, just a minute too long, and as I started to ask if he would consider filling in for a couple of months, the sky exploded with color and cheers erupted loud enough that I couldn't even hear myself. For the next ten minutes, the colors filling the sky mesmerized me. The crackle of the gold ones that fell in the shape of a weeping willow took all my worries away. They were my favorite and if they chose to do a show with just those, I would be the happiest person alive.

The finale started and I barely registered Declan's hand grazing my leg before making its way into my own hand when we heard a loud buzzing sound forcing its way toward us. It was so loud we could almost feel it. Declan and I stood and jumped off the side of the bleachers, followed by Clyde, working our way toward the sound. We just reached the gate when a loud pop filled the air and half the green went dark. Declan pulled the metal gate open with the toe of his boot giving all of us plenty of room to walk through. "Don't touch the gate."

All the rides and booths closed before the fireworks started but the lights were supposed to stay on so the workers could clean up and the visitors could see to make their way off the grounds. Directly inside the gate we just passed through was the teacup ride where Diesel found the button on the first day. "Oh, it smells like smoke and burnt hair." I waved my hand in front of my face and Declan used the flashlight on his phone to guide us around.

"Maybe Diesel was on to something yesterday." He turned the light toward the back of the ride and we could see smoke rising from every outlet. Diesel mewled and scrambled in Declan's arms, but he held tight. "You're not going anywhere this time." He passed the cat off to Clyde and leaned just slightly over the second gate that separated the electrical equipment from any pedestrians. His flashlight beam landed on a pair of shoes sticking out from the corner of the ride. "Not again. Dakota, call Alex. Have him meet us over here."

"I know who that is. I recognize his shoes."

Arrowsmith

"Clyde, go over and make sure no one else tries to come in where we just did. Do not touch the gate." He turned to face me. "Who is it?"

"Anything we can help y'all with?" A man with a strong, southern accent came up beside Declan, interrupting our conversation. We could barely see his face.

"No, thank you. The detective is on his way. Just get yourself and your family and friends out safely."

By the time Alex arrived, Joe, Nick, Wyatt, and Falcon had already set up a human barrier to stop people from trying to see what was happening. Kerry and Nikki offered to bring Fiona home and the security team for the fair brought over some flood lights so Alex could see better. He ignored the guys who were keeping everyone away and walked directly over to me. "How is it even possible that it's you, again?"

"We were sitting on the bleachers at the high school. As soon as we heard the electrical buzz, we ran over to see what was happening. You'd think you would be grateful that we have the situation under control."

"Really, I'd prefer to not have so many people die in my town. The fact that you and your friends are around every time it happens doesn't make me feel any better, even if you are trying to help out."

"Well, would it help if I told you we found a clue yesterday that may help you with this one?"

His body visibly tensed. "This looks to me like it was an accident. But if you're withholding evidence to a crime, it may not look good for you."

I drew in a deep breath to calm myself. "This may not have been an accident, but what we found wouldn't have been considered evidence until now."

"That doesn't make any sense and if you'll excuse me, I have a job to do." He tried to turn away, but I grabbed his shoulder and turned him back to me.

"Listen to me. You know yesterday Declan and I opened the shop for a few hours. There were so many people standing outside, looking through the windows, we thought we could curb their curiosity if we opened for a while. There was one guy who came in that had no interest in actually getting a tattoo. He just wanted photos and video for his crime podcast. He's actually pretty popular among the true crime enthusiasts. We pulled up his website last night but all he had posted was a teaser that said that Mack guy wasn't who we thought he was and he told his listeners to stay tuned for more information. Two days ago, the fair opened late because the whole back half of the green didn't have any power. This area." I gestured with my hand in case he wasn't sure what I was referring to. "When we finally got in, I was walking around in this area and Diesel went crazy, jumped out of my arms, and ran back here. He pulled a fancy button out of one of the outlets back here. At the time, we just assumed maybe it was part of the reason the power wasn't working."

"What is a fancy button?"

"Like a shirt button. But it had a green stone in it. And Mack introduced himself to Clyde as a jeweler so it makes sense that he might have something fancy like that."

"Right. But that's purely a coincidence since Mack was dead before the fair opened."

"Yes. But *he* wasn't." I pointed to the shoes on the corner. "Those shoes belong to the guy who runs the crime podcast. I remember them specifically because, of course, they're ridiculous, but he also kept tapping his foot while I was tattooing him and I kept looking at his feet because it was annoying me."

He rolled his eyes. "So, you think a jeweler and a guy who runs a podcast are somehow linked? I don't have time for this."

"Yes, because he said Mack wasn't who we all thought he was. Maybe he had real evidence about who Mack really was."

"Mack was already dead." He put emphasis on every syllable as he spoke.

"Maybe there's someone out there who doesn't want people to know who Mack really was." I responded to him by also putting emphasis on every word. I didn't like the way he was speaking to me, so I gave it right back to him.

"I'm going to need that button." He walked away and his body language told me he wasn't happy about our conversation. That was okay. I had no doubt he'd be knocking on my door first thing in the morning and I had a lot more to tell him.

Chapter 9

I was glad we had an early night again. The guys stayed to run crowd control for Alex, which was more than I probably would have done for him, but once they got back to my house, things quieted down fast. A small part of me wanted to ask Declan to sleep in the living room with everyone else but a larger part of me couldn't bear the thought of sleeping in my bed without him next to me. As soon as I laid down, I turned my back to him and moved all the way to the edge of the bed. I still didn't know if I imagined him curled around me or not, but I had been nervous around him all day. I fell asleep to the thought of him grabbing my hand on the bleachers replaying in my head.

Just after six, I woke to a sharp knock on my front door. I groaned and rolled out of bed, throwing a hoodie over my head as I went to the door. I knew it would be Alex, but I didn't want him to knock again. The last thing I wanted was a bunch of grumpy men around me all day. I opened the door and waved Alex in, silently gesturing for him to watch where he walked so he didn't step on anyone.

When I got to the kitchen, I didn't even look in his direction. I immediately began brewing a pot of coffee.

"Well, your house certainly looks comfortable."

"Yeah, I didn't think about the fact that it's the busiest weekend of the summer. I invited them all and then realized none of them had a place to stay."

"It looks like you're running a homeless shelter."

"There's no need to be rude and it does not. It was either this or they were camping in my back yard." I slammed an empty coffee mug on the table in front of him without asking if he wanted any and crossed my arms over my chest as I leaned against the counter. "I assume you're here for the button?"

"You assume correctly. I, um, may also need Declan's help with something." He looked down at the table and sighed.

"What do you want him for?"

"I just need help with something that I think he can do faster than my team can."

I poured coffee in both cups and offered him the bottle of milk which he accepted. "Well, he's still sleeping, so you'll have to wait."

"I'm awake. I don't know how anyone slept through that knocking." He poured himself coffee and sat at the table with Diesel sitting on his shoulder. He stared at Alex. I knew he wouldn't give him the satisfaction of asking what he needed help with. He was going to make Alex ask.

I pulled the button out of the drawer I put it in last night and placed it on the table. "If you think you have time for it, we have some information that may help you."

He glared at me, knowing I was pushing him to ask Declan for help. "Fine. I'll give you time in a minute but before we get to that, I need to ask Declan for his help."

Declan's lips curled up at the corners. It was barely noticeable, but I saw it. He still stared at him without saying a word.

"I understand you do some sort of security thing, is that correct?"

"Some security thing, yeah. I set up security systems for people on their computers and their phones. It's amazing how many people don't know how easy it is for people to access their information."

"Does your security expertise ever go into having to unlock accounts or gain access to computers or websites?"

Declan's jaw tightened and he drew a deep breath in before answering. "I certainly hope you're not asking for my help at the same time you're accusing me of hacking into people's accounts. That's not what I do."

"But you can do it?" Alex's eyes grew wide and hopeful.

Declan rolled his eyes. "Can you just tell me what you need?"

"I need to get into Shawn's phone and I need access to his websites to see what he has stored on them."

"And Shawn would be...?"

"The victim from last night. He got stuck running the teacup ride and he wasn't happy about it. I haven't spent much time at the fair, but I guess he was spending more time away from the ride than he was running it. Other workers had to keep stepping in for him."

"I thought the podcast was his job?"

"It is, was, is, but the fair was his second job for the weekend."

"Ah. So, you want to me access his phone so you can see if you can figure out why he wanted the job there and to see if he's hiding anything additional about Mack based on what Dakota told you last night?"

"Exactly."

"I can't believe I'm going to say this, but as long as I have a guarantee that I'm not going to get slammed for hacking into his phone, I'll help you."

"You have my word."

Because Alex got what he came for, he sat and listened to everything we had to tell him. I reiterated what Shawn had posted in his video. I reminded him where we found the button and told him that Elliott admitted to knowing Mack. I filled him in on what Brooks does for a living. Alex took notes and thanked us for the information. We told him we'd be by the station as soon as we got ready to leave.

"I can't believe he had the nerve to ask for my help."

"I can't believe you're going to do it. He comes over and tries to blame me and our friends for murder and then asks for help because you can do it faster than the people he has on staff to do it."

"The only reason I agreed is because I want the murderer caught. He told me last time his tech team isn't from here. He has to send the items out to have them looked at. It could take weeks depending on how much they have going on."

"I guess you're right. Maybe this time he'll realize that none of us are capable of murder."

"I think you give him too much credit."

We spent three hours at the station going through all of Shawn's files. By the time we finished, we only had two new pieces of information. One was more helpful than the other. He was right when he said Mack wasn't who he claimed to be. He wasn't a jeweler; he was a private investigator. He had a license in all states except Hawaii and South Dakota. That was helpful information. We found a lot of pictures and video footage he took both inside and outside my shop, but he took them all during the day I tattooed him. We didn't find anything related to the job at the fair, even in his search history. The second interesting thing we found was a picture of a bracelet that I was sure had been auctioned two days before. I couldn't get a clear enough image. It looked like he took the picture while he was walking by the item, trying not to draw attention to himself.

    Declan stayed logged in to all the sites on Shawn's phone and disabled the screen lock so Alex could access it again if he needed to. We made notes and walked him through everything we found before leaving the station. We barely got a thank you.

    Diesel had been asleep in my bag the whole time we were inside but once we hit sunlight, he poked his head out. We decided to take my Jeep today and Alex gave us permission to leave it in the parking lot while we went over to the fair. Trying to park near the green was a nightmare. I set Diesel on the roof and threw my bag inside before tossing the keys to Declan. "Oh!" I took a deep breath. I ran to the other side of the vehicle. "Can you pull up a picture of all the items they auctioned the other day? I need to see a good picture of that bracelet."

Declan pulled up the list and zoomed in on what looked like an ID bracelet. "This one?"

I grabbed his phone from his hand. "Yes. You see that lion engraved on it right there? That matches the ring Elliott had on the day we met him. How much did this one sell for? Did they post the prices anywhere?" I handed him back his phone.

I watched his eyes grow wide. "They did. It sold for eighteen- thousand, five hundred."

"Right. That was the most expensive item, I think. Does it say who bought it?"

"No. But I bet we can find out." He pulled Diesel from the roof where the cat perched in the sun and we finally started our journey to the green.

Chapter 10

Declan and I spent two hours trying to find anyone with information about the auction, but we didn't have any luck. We decided if we were going to find someone to ask, we would do better if we weren't looking. It was way past time for lunch and we went in two different directions, to get what we wanted. It was the last day of the fair and we both had a few items we wanted to try. I took Diesel with me and walked toward the back by the rides where I knew the pizza truck was set up.

     I had just gotten in line when Diesel started with that low growl that always sent a shiver through me. He didn't try to get away, but I could feel the direction he was looking. I looked over to find Elliott and Brooks mid-conversation and it looked like they were both angry. They were standing away from the crowd, both red-faced and waving their hands in the air. I decided to pretend I didn't notice how heated their argument was I left the line and walked right up to both of them. "Hey. Long time, no see. You both getting your fill of the fair?" I could tell they were both trying to control their anger and not tell me I was being rude by interrupting.

"Yeah, we sure are. Um, I was actually about to go get something to eat. Brooks, I'll catch up with you." Elliott walked away as fast as he could without trying to make it obvious.

"Just think, maybe this time next year, you'll be here permanently." I smiled at him, but he wasn't looking at me. He was too busy watching which direction Elliott was heading in. "Have you had lunch? I was about to grab a slice of pizza if you'd like to join me."

He finally turned his attention to me and stuttered. "Uhh..." He pulled his watch from his pocket and I gasped when I saw it. He saw me looking at the watch and his face fell. "I, uh, need to go make a phone call." He practically ran in the same direction Elliott went.

"That was weird, huh? Do you want to get a slice of pizza with me?" Diesel mewled. It took almost forty-five minutes to get my food and I guessed Declan was having the same experience because he hadn't come to find me yet. I was hoping to talk to him soon. After seeing the watch Brooks carried in the daylight, I knew what I needed was right in front of me. I just couldn't place it.

After I ate, I moved to the outside of the grounds, hoping it would be easier to find Declan. Watching everywhere except straight ahead, I slammed into what felt like a wall, wearing a Hawaiian shirt. "Elliott. I'm so sorry. I wasn't paying attention to where I was walking."

"No harm done. Are you okay?"

"Yes, thank you." Embarrassment aside, I was glad I ran into him. "You didn't look like you were enjoying the conversation with Brooks earlier..." I couldn't help but glance down at his hand. "Did it have anything to do with your grandfather's ring?"

He took a step backward and his eyes grew large. "How much did you hear?" His voice had the faintest tremble.

"I didn't hear anything. But, the ring you wear has the same lion engraved on it as his pocket watch. And if I'm not mistaken, a bracelet with that exact lion was sold at the auction two days ago. You can't believe that's a coincidence." His breathing was growing heavy, I could see his shoulders rising and falling with each breath.

"He's been trying to buy it from me for years. I won't do it. I can't." He shook his head and glanced to each side. "Dakota, you don't understand what you think you know. Pretend you never put these things together and keep your mouth shut...for your own safety." He pushed by me and walked away without so much as a glance behind him.

I pulled out my phone to text Declan and heard my name being called. Diesel growled and he pushed off my shoulder. I turned just in time to see him jump on Brooks. Brooks raised his hand; I saw it curl into a fist and everything went black.

When I opened my eyes, I knew immediately that I was in one of the beach cabins. All of them were set up the exact same way. I tried to sit up, but Brooks had tied me to the bed. I didn't see Brooks anywhere but sitting on the nightstand, the ID bracelet that sold at the auction was facing me. I wasn't sure who purchased it, but I did know it wasn't Brooks. I also knew now that his watch was part of this same set. I didn't know how many pieces there were, but I knew there were at least three: a ring, a bracelet, and a watch. Together, they must be worth a fortune.

I heard the door squeak open and Brooks came into the room and sat in the wooden chair opposite the bed. "I knew you were going to trouble the minute I met you."

I was feeling awfully brave for someone who couldn't move. "What happened to your accent?"

"That's not important. What is important is how much you know."

"Well, I'm guessing the main reason you're out here is because you want to complete your set.

And I can see you already have the watch and bracelet. All you need is the ring, right?"

"You're too smart for your own good. How'd you know?"

"Well, Shawn helped before you killed him. He had video on his phone stating that Mack wasn't who he claimed to be. A separate video told us he was actually a PI. And Shawn had a picture of that bracelet," I nodded my head toward the nightstand, "on his phone. The day I met Elliott, I noticed his ring and commented on it. But it was when I saw your watch, I knew it must have been you."

He leaned back in the chair and crossed his arms. "And what makes you think it was me and not Elliott? He had one of the pieces, too. You only knew about my watch. You didn't know I had the bracelet."

"Because the bracelet sold for a lot of money. But that watch, in working condition, has to be the most valuable item. There's no way you would consider selling it. And since you own an antiques store, it stands to reason you would have some sort of bill of sale for it. Which means you would be able to forge a bill of sale much easier than someone who doesn't own a shop."

He stared at me but didn't say anything.

"The only part of the puzzle I'm missing is why you had to kill Mack. Where does he fit in to all this?"

"Since you asked so nicely, I'll tell you. There's another buyer who has been trying to get a hold of these pieces for years. He sent Mack to my shop a few years ago with some counterfeit items as a means to get into my shop. I threatened him and told him to never come back. I don't deal with counterfeit goods, I never have. Mack has been on this collector's payroll for years and they hired him to track down these items. Knowing I would also be here, I had to assume he would come after me once he secured the bracelet. So, I took care of him first."

The only window in the bedroom was on the opposite wall, behind the wooden chair. I could see movement outside but didn't want to bring attention to it. "But Mack was only a PI, not a murderer."

"People change and he stood to get a lot of money if he was able to recover these pieces." He crossed his ankle over one knee, almost like he was enjoying the conversation, completely at ease.

"Did you really kill Shawn because you thought his podcast would lead detectives back to you?"

"I wasn't too worried about it, but when I realized he was working at the fair, it was too easy. I just short-circuited the control board so when he turned off the lights at the end of the night, it would be lights out for him, too."

I didn't know what else to say but I needed to distract him. "I guess that makes sense. It's always best to tie up any loose ends."

He nodded. "Yes. Loose ends are always a problem. Which is why I'm so conflicted with what to do with you."

Brooks didn't get to finish his thought. Alex kicked the door to the cabin in and ran in with his gun drawn. Brooks didn't have time to react because the cabins are so small.

I didn't see what happened next because I focused on Declan. He pulled his knife from his pocket and sliced the ropes, freeing my hands, and moved on to my feet. "Thank you."

He pulled me into his arms and hugged me tighter than he ever has before.

"How did you know where to find me?"

"Wonder Diesel. At some point, he must have attacked Brooks because he ran over to me and Falcon and dropped a piece of that hideous shirt in my hands."

I looked over just as Alex was walking Brooks out the door in handcuffs. "The bucking broncos."

"Yup. Falcon told me he recognized it from the night at your house."

"That cat is something else."

"He sure is."

Chapter 11

I decided not to go back to the fair that night. I wanted nothing more than to go home and rest. Declan and I made some sandwiches and sat on the front porch when it started to get dark outside. It wouldn't be the same, but I knew I would be able to see most of the fireworks from my front yard. We finished eating just as they started.

"So, last night during the fireworks, you asked me a question, and now I need to do the same to you."

"Oh? Okay. Do your worst."

"I know you have a full schedule this week but is there any way you might consider watching Diesel for me for a few days?"

I had to laugh. "Is that a serious question? You don't even need to ask that; you could just leave him. You know I'll take care of him."

"Aren't you curious why I need to leave him?"

"Of course. I would have gotten around to asking you eventually. Why do you need to leave him?"

"I think I need to go home to pick up a few things and it'll be easier if I don't have to worry about him."

I stared at him for a minute, confused by what he was saying.

"Last time I was here, I didn't want to leave. I know you can take care of yourself but I worried about you every day that I was gone. After this week, I'm not sure I can do that again. If it's okay with you, I'd like to stick around for a while longer."

I didn't know what to say. I tried, but nothing came out when I opened my mouth.

"Well, you know I always tell you there's never a dull moment when you're around and I think I'd like to keep the excitement up for a while, sans murder. Maybe I'll go back to tattooing. Of course, if you decided you don't want another artist, I understand."

I don't know what got into me, but I leaned in and kissed him just as the fireworks finale was starting. When I backed away, I leaned my head on his shoulder. "I would love for you to stay."

Traditional will Tell

A Dakota Maddison Tattoo Shop Mystery
Book 3

Chapter 1

It was finally time for the event I have been looking forward to the most since I arrived six months ago. Every September, the town sponsors a pet adoption event. This town doesn't know how to do anything small. Aside from the adoptions themselves, they also raise money for surrounding local shelters by hosting a silent auction, having a petting zoo for a minimal fee, and this year, they are giving hot air balloon rides over the lake. All proceeds go to the shelters.

Declan and I both entered items and services for the silent auction. He had been in town for a little over two months now and I felt like things were finally falling into place. I hadn't seen either Alex or Annette for over a month, Declan was working at the shop part-time, mainly taking walk-ins, and I hadn't seen or been associated with any dead bodies since July.

It was Wednesday afternoon and I had no plans other than sitting on the back patio, reading. The autumn air had finally hit and a cool breeze made it's way across the yard. Leaves were starting to change colors, showcasing maroons, golds, and bright oranges. As much as I love the heat of summer, fall is the most visually appealing.

Declan had taken my Jeep earlier in the day and I heard him pull into the driveway as soon as I opened my book. He joined me on the patio and sat in the chair next to me. "I picked something up while I was out today."

I stared at him waiting to continue.

"You know Nick works with foster animals, right? He has a lot of connections, including with some of the shelters that will bringing cats and dogs this weekend." He paused, waiting for a response that I didn't give him. "Anyway, I know you and how you are when it comes to animals. I have no doubt you'd want to bring home every animal see so I got something to deter you."

I curled my top lip, wondering where he was going with this but still didn't verbally respond.

"Come with me. I need your help getting it out of the car." I followed him in silence having no idea what he could possibly have done. "I know you refuse to buy a pet outright from a breeder, but I also know how much you've wanted one of these. Before you yell, he's adopted, not bought." He opened the door and I poked my head around him to see the smallest, cutest, little boxer I've ever seen in my life staring at me from the passenger's seat.

Author's Note

When you are finished reading, if you do not keep physical books, please consider donating your copy to your local library for their book sale or to your local prison book program.

Author's Bio

Trish recently moved across the country where she found her forever home, enjoying the desert sunshine and wildlife all year long. She was born and raised in a small town in northern Connecticut. Growing up, she was always fascinated by unsolved mysteries and true crimes as well as the psychological elements behind them. As an avid reader, her go to books are thriller/suspense, true crime, and cozy mysteries.

Made in the USA
Middletown, DE
28 April 2025

74845138R00071